Kids vs. Nature

Book 1

Surviving
Moose Lake

Written by:
Karl Steam

Illustrated by:
Joshua Lagman

Contents

Surviving
Moose Lake

Chapter 1
The Beginning

I still remember when it all started. It was the last week of sixth grade, the morning John Marten stuck his foot in front of Tyler. Tyler fell and a deck of playing cards scattered across the hallway.

John didn't even stop to enjoy his evil deed, but called over his shoulder, "Watch where you're going Blob."

It's not just John who calls him that. Tyler's been nicknamed "The Blob" since second grade. Why? I don't know. Probably because he's overweight, wears sweat pants every day, and dips whatever the lunch ladies serve us in ranch dressing. Even French toast! Nasty, right?

That's the main reason he sits alone in the cafeteria; no one can stand to watch him eat. Not that he seems to mind. It gives him plenty of room to spread his cards out—the kind that have pictures of wizards and dragons on them.

They're probably the same cards that scattered across the hallway when John tripped him. Tyler crawled on the floor, trying to pick them up before too many people stepped on them. I tip-toed around the cards the best I could, but the hall was busy and narrow.

John was still smiling as we entered our classroom. I knew John wasn't a very nice guy, but lately, my best friend Mark has been hanging around him a lot. Since me and Mark pretty much do everything together, I've been spending more time around John too, so now I really know just how mean he can be.

Like normal, Melisa Bay was already done with the bell-work questions. My teacher, Mrs. Emmons, always has questions written on the chalk board when we come to class. We're supposed to sit and answer the questions right away so that they're finished by the time the bell rings, which is why she calls them "bell-work questions."

I don't have a problem sitting when we get to class, but I refuse to work on the questions. They don't seem fair. Why should kids need to work before the bell? Classes are long enough already. *After* the bell is when class should start. *Before* the bell rings should be our time to talk and relax.

While waiting for class to start, I wondered what things would be like when sixth grade was over. Graduating from elementary school seemed to be a big deal to everyone else. There would be a graduation ceremony and everything, but I couldn't understand why going from sixth grade to seventh grade was so different than the end of any other school year.

I tried to imagine what middle school would be like. School without recess didn't sound fun. I wondered if there would be a lot of homework and if middle school teachers used bell-work problems too. I was feeling more and more nervous about life after sixth grade when I noticed a large trunk in the corner of the room. It was big, black, and looked heavy.

Chapter 2
My Group

It turns out big, black, heavy looking trunks like that come from organizations that feel bad for kids that go to lame schools like Northview Elementary. Since my school never brings students on field trips, places like the Black Wagon Science Museum send us trunks full of exhibits instead.

I'll admit, the trunk wasn't that bad, at least compared to listening to Mrs. Emmons talk about the difference between physical traits and physical characteristics for an entire class period. The trunk had a lot of cool things inside for us to look at. Plus, Mrs. Emmons set everything into different stations, which means we could get out of our seats and move from one place to the next.

The bad thing was we had to work in groups, and we couldn't pick our groups.

"It's important to work with new people," Mrs. Emmons said, when I suggested that we choose our partners.

She might as well have said, "Josh, I'm going to put you with a boring group, so you don't talk with Mark too much."

It's true, I get a little distracted around Mark, but being paired with two girls and Tyler (The Blob) should be considered a cruel and unusual punishment. On the bright side though, one of the girls was Katie Roberts. She's unarguably the best-looking girl in school and pretty much perfect in every way. On the down side, I feel awkward around Katie. On a steeper downside, the other girl was Melisa Bay. Bossy, know-it-all are the only words needed to describe Melisa.

We sat in a circle around our station. Melisa did most of the work, which was using a classification system to figure out what trees different kinds of leaves and needles came from. That's right, not only was I stuck with a bad group, but I couldn't even start at one of the fun stations.

Katie ignored everything the group did and looked across the room. Mrs. Emmons was busy helping Mark's group unfold some animal hides. Katie pulled a phone from her pocket and texted one of her gazillion friends.

"Hey, is that the new Xylo," Tyler asked.

"Ah, yea."

"Can I see it?"

Katie glanced at Mrs. Emmons before passing the phone to Tyler. "Just don't get it taken away."

"You guys, focus," Melisa said. She pinched a leaf by the stem and held it in front of my face. "Do you think this is from a red oak or a white oak?"

That's when I had an idea that changed our lives forever. "Does your phone get internet?" I asked.

Katie rolled her eyes. "What do you think?"

"Let's look up the answers," I said.

Melisa crossed her arms while Tyler searched the web.

"Identifying leaves," Tyler mumbled as he typed in the search bar. He clicked a few links and shook his head. "There's a lot of trees to search through."

"It's cheating anyways," Melisa scolded.

"Wait a second," Tyler turned the phone, so Katie could see the screen. "There's a nature identification app. You can download a free version for a week."

"Try it," Katie said.

Tyler tapped a dark blue icon that had a firefly in the center. "Hang on. It's loading."

He tapped the phone a few more times, then something strange happened. The whole screen went dark. A firefly appeared in the center. Its tail blinked on and off, making a light that grew brighter with each pulse. Soon the whole screen turned a greenish-gold color, and a light sprang from the phone. It was like having a thousand yellow camera flashes go off at once.

Naturally, I closed my eyes. I think I even threw my arms in the air to block the light. Everything happened too fast for me to really remember. All I know is that when I opened my eyes again, I was surrounded by golden green smoke, except I don't think it was smoke because of the way it glowed and swirled. Whatever that stuff was, it faded away fast. Like it evaporated or something, and that's when I realized I wasn't in Northview Elementary anymore.

Chapter 3
What the...

Can you remember the last time you wet your bed? Well, I can remember the last time I did. (Don't worry, I was four at the time.) I went to the bathroom, lifted the toilet seat, and started to go. Then the next thing I knew a warm sensation was trickling around my legs. That's when I realized I wasn't in the bathroom at all but still lying in my bed. I was only dreaming that I was in the bathroom.

Well, that's kind of how I felt as the glowing smoke disappeared. One moment I could have sworn I was in Mrs. Emmons' room. The next second, I was somewhere completely different. Tyler, Katie, and Melisa were there too. By the looks on their faces, I could tell they felt exactly the same way I did.

We were all positioned as we had been around our station, but now we were sitting on top of dirty twigs. There was a lake on one side of us, but trees and bushes were everywhere else. I can't tell you exactly what kinds of trees were in the forest because I really wasn't paying attention when Melisa was doing the classifying. All I know is that half of the trees had leaves and the rest had needles.

Our clothes were different too. Well, I mean they were different than the clothes we had been wearing at school. Now we had matching outfits which included jeans, leather shoes, and a T-shirt.

Katie picked her phone off the ground and wiped dirt away from the screen. "What'd you do?" she asked Tyler.

"I didn't do anything," he said.

Melisa glanced at her clothing. She pointed to the firefly icon on her shirt. "Obviously, you did," she said.

Katie stood and held the phone above her head. She turned different directions, trying to find a signal. She dialed a number and put the phone to her ear. "I can't even call for help," she said. Katie shoved the phone into Tyler's soft stomach. "Take us back."

Tyler hesitated.

"Now!"

Tyler took the phone and fiddled with it. "I don't even know what happened. It just downloaded, and suddenly we're here."

"Didn't you click something after it loaded," I asked.

"Yea, the user agreement," he said.

"Give me that." Melisa pulled the phone from Tyler. She tapped the screen a couple times before stopping to read something. Her finger slid across the phone to scroll further down the page. Melisa glared at Tyler. "I can't believe you hit 'Accept' without actually reading the Terms and Conditions."

Tyler shrugged. "Nobody reads those things. It's fine."

Chapter 4
Exploring

While Melisa tried to figure out how to get us back to Mrs. Emmons' class, I decided to explore. I walked closer to the lake. Tyler and Katie followed.

"Maybe someone has a cabin close by," I said. But there wasn't a boat or house in sight.

The lake's shoreline only had trees, rocks, and more trees. I knew Katie was listening to me, so I tried to think of something else to say.

"Everything's so still," I said.

It was true too. Ripples drifted across the lake, but nothing else moved. In Columbus, Ohio, people go indoors if they want their world to be still. Outside, there are always cars driving back and forth, people jogging in the parks, airplanes, bikes... You get the picture.

"Yea," Katie agreed, "it's peaceful."

We stood there for a while, just soaking in the great outdoors when Tyler yelled, "AAAAAHHHHHHHHHHHHHHHHHHHH!"

Katie screamed, and Tyler yelled some more. We stepped closer to each other and looked around the forest.

"What is it?" I asked.

Tyler's eyes were open wider than usual. "I don't know," he said.

Katie pushed Tyler away from her, "Then why are you yelling?

"It was so quiet, I wanted to see if my voice would echo. Then you started yelling, and I thought you saw a bear or something."

Melisa ran to us, then slowed to a walk. "What happened?" she asked.

Katie rolled her eyes. She stomped past Melisa. "I can't believe I'm stuck here with you losers."

Ouch, the honest truth. Let's just say that you'd never find people like Tyler, Melisa, or me sitting at the same table as Katie in the cafeteria. If it weren't for us being assigned to the same group, she wouldn't bother talking to us at all.

"You guys, I think I know how to get back," Melisa said. "One of the statements in the *Terms and Conditions* said that anyone who uses the App's free trial agrees to complete all of the missions that are assigned to them." Melisa had emphasized "Terms and Conditions" and glared at Tyler.

Tyler stared at the ground. "I'm sorry, okay I didn't mean to."

"It's not like he did it on purpose," I said.

Melisa glanced at me then back at Tyler. Her posture softened. "I know, just try to be more careful next time."

"So, what's the mission," I asked.

Honestly, I was excited to find out. It felt like we were going to be spies or secret agents. A mysterious mission seemed like a lot more fun than Mrs. Emmons' class.

Melisa tapped the phone, then turned it for us to see.

"We have to shoot a moose," I asked. "With what?"

"Look, I don' know. That's just the way it sounds." Melisa answered.

"We're going to be hunters," Tyler said.

Up until that point in my life, the only thing I can remember hunting was a fly that was in my house. I would wait for it to land and creep up on it. But every time I tried to hit it with the fly swatter, it seemed to move out of the way at the very last instant. Then it would fly from one room to the next before landing somewhere else.

Let's just say that I'm not always the most patient person. After a while, instead of letting it land, I ran after it, swinging the swatter through the air. The more I missed, the angrier I became. And the angrier I became, the harder I swung.

Two knocked over picture frames and one crying little sister later, my mom confiscated the swatter. By that time, the fly was buzzing straight into our screen door, over and over and over again. My mom opened the door a crack. The fly buzzed outside as if it didn't have a care in the world.

Needless to say, my one hunting experience was an epic failure.

Chapter 5
The Hunt Begins

We figured the best way to find a moose was to find its tracks first. Honestly, we didn't know what moose tracks would look like, but agreed they'd have to be big. We split up to cover more ground, except for Katie, who found a log to sit on. She didn't want anything to do with moose hunting.

We weren't looking very long before Tyler pointed to the edge of the lake and yelled, "Hey, there's a monkey around here!"

Melisa and I walked over to look.

"Monkeys don't live in North America," she said.

"Yea, we're in a forest, not a jungle," I agreed.

As we came closer, I couldn't believe my eyes. There really were little monkey tracks pressed into the mud by the lake. Each track had five fingers and a palm, like tiny human hand prints.

"What kind of place is this?" Melisa asked. "This doesn't make any sense. I thought we were in Canada or something."

I shrugged. "Let's see where they go."

We followed the tracks. They were easy to see in the mud, but occasionally disappeared wherever the monkey walked through a patch of grass. We had to go around all the bushes and fallen trees the monkey had been able to crawl under. That made tracking slow, but it was still fun.

"Look at that," Melisa said.

I was so busy looking at the ground to see that we were walking right up to a canoe. All the bushes made it hard to see from where we first appeared, but now that we were closer, it looked as if someone had laid it there for us to find.

The first thing I did was check to see if there were any paddles next to it. There were two tucked underneath, and a couple lifejackets. As I pulled the paddles out, I noticed a bag too. "Check this out," I said.

The bag was black, and made of a thick, rubber coated fabric. There were two shoulder straps attached to it, which made it look like a really strange backpack.

Something inside rattled as I pulled it out from beneath the canoe.

I was just about to reach inside of the open end when Melisa asked, "Did you see this?"

She stepped closer and pointed to a firefly on the front of the bag. It was the same symbol on the app and our t-shirts.

I know being transported out of a classroom isn't exactly normal, but seeing that symbol on the backpack sent chills running down my spine. For some reason, it creeped me out.

I pulled a metal pot out of the bag. Inside the pot was a box of matches and a pocket knife. The only other things in the bag were a few ropes and two canteens, and you can probably guess what logo was printed on the side of the canteens.

"No food?" Tyler asked.

"And nothing to hunt a moose with," I added.

Tyler held up the pocket knife. "We have this." He put the knife in his pocket.

I shook my head. "You can't hunt a moose with that. It's too small."

"Well, it's better than nothing," Melisa said.

I tried to figure out how to close the bag. It only had two clips attached to the top of it, so I decided it must be designed to stay open.

Melisa went to the front of the canoe and tried pulling it closer to the lake. It didn't move. "A little help would be nice," she said. "The monkey tracks show up best wherever the ground is wet. If we paddle close to shore, maybe we'll see some moose tracks in the mud too. It'll be easier than walking through the brush."

Chapter 6
Off We Go

It took all three of us to flip the canoe over and push it in the lake. Then Melisa went to get Katie. We didn't want to leave her alone. After all, if there were moose and monkeys around, who knows what else might be in the forest.

We put our lifejackets on and crawled into the canoe. I went in first and sat in the front seat with a paddle. Melisa and Katie climbed in next but sat on the floor because there weren't enough seats for everyone. Then Tyler sat on the back seat.

After we were all settled, Tyler and I began to paddle. The only problem was we didn't go anywhere. The front of the canoe moved from side to side, but that was it. Between the water being too shallow and Tyler being too heavy, the back of the canoe was stuck in the sand. Tyler tried pushing away from shore with his paddle, but it was no use.

"You've got to be kidding me," Katie said. "This whole day stinks."

"Everyone just lean together. All we need is a little momentum," Melisa said. "Forward on three. One."

I grabbed the sides of the canoe.

"Two."

I leaned backward.

"Three."

I pulled my body forward as fast as I could. The canoe budged. It wasn't much, but it scooted forward enough for Tyler to push the back end into deeper water with his paddle. I could tell by the way we were smoothly gliding that the whole canoe was now floating.

"Go straight," Katie scolded. "Stay close to shore."

The canoe had been pointed in the right direction to skim along the shoreline, but the more me and Tyler paddled, the more the canoe turned toward the middle of the lake. I tried to paddle on the other side of the canoe, but it didn't seem to help.

"Josh, just paddle and stop trying to steer. It's the person in the back that does that," Katie said. "Tyler, paddle on the right side and it'll turn left. Paddle on the left, and it'll go right."

Tyler tried a couple more strokes but looked confused.

Katie's eyebrows narrowed. "Come on you guys; it's not rocket science."

"I'd like to see you try," Melisa challenged.

"Give me your paddle," Katie demanded. She repositioned herself from a sitting to kneeling position and took the paddle from Tyler. "Josh just paddle straight."

Katie paddled too. At first, it didn't look like anything changed, but after a few strokes, the front of the canoe turned away from the center of the lake. Soon, we were traveling along the shoreline. Sometimes, Katie switched which side she paddled on. Other times, she dragged her paddle in the water to steer. "See, I know what I'm doing," she said. "I canoe every summer at the resort my family goes to."

Melisa crossed her arms and turned so that she could watch for tracks.

Chapter 7
On the Trail

At first, there were more monkey tracks, but eventually they went away. We were halfway around the lake when I saw different tracks— bigger tracks.

"Here we go," I said, and pointed at them with the tip of my paddle.

Katie steered us to shore. The front of the canoe landed on the beach, and we climbed out.

The tracks were big alright. Man, oh man, were they big. We followed them into the forest. Unlike monkey tracks, which didn't show up well in grass, the moose tracks could still be seen. The moose was heavier, so its feet sank deep into the ground.

At first, it was a competition to see who could find the next moose track. We'd run in front of the others, find which way the trail was going, and yell, "This way. Follow me."

It was Tyler who eventually pointed out that we should probably be quieter while hunting for moose. After that, we walked slowly, whispered, and occasionally paused to listen for anything moving in the woods. Ironically, it was also Tyler who had a hard time being quiet. He completely tripped over a log and stumbled over a tree root.

We had been walking a long time when the trail entered a swamp. The further we went, the more it felt like we were walking on a sponge. Muddy water squished from the ground with each step we took.

Eventually, the trail led to a pond. It was obvious where the moose had swum across. It left a dark line through the algae. The reeds on the far end were still bent to the sides too.

Melisa struggled to lift her foot out of the mud. "You guys, we can't go in there," she said. "We'll get stuck."

She was right too. That was as far as we could follow the trail.

Chapter 8
Something Sweet

If there's one thing I learned, it's that tracking an animal forward is entertaining, but following tracks backward is incredibly boring. Every step you take feels like a step further away from the animal you're hunting. After a while, I really wasn't looking for tracks anymore. It seemed like too much work. I just followed everyone else back to the lake.

I was zoning out, sort of like I do when things get really boring in Mrs. Emmons' class, when I bumped into Melisa. She had stopped walking and was bending over to look at something on the ground.

"Hey, watch it," she said. Melisa bent over again and pulled a berry off a short plant. She used a finger to roll it around the palm of her hand. "I think I found a blueberry."

"Eat it," I said.

She shook her head. "No. I don't know for sure. It just looks like one."

"Well, just taste it then."

Melisa held the berry toward me. "You taste it."

I wasn't about to be a human guinea pig, so I didn't bother to take it from her.

"I'll try it," Tyler said, and Melisa set it in his hand.

"Wait a minute," I said. "We downloaded that App to help us identify plants. We might as well use it."

"You're right," Melisa said.

Katie took her phone out and typed "blueberry" into the app's search bar. A moment later, a couple images appeared. One was a close-up picture of the berry itself and the other a picture of the leaves that grow on the plant. It went on to describe blueberries and how to distinguish them from other poisonous berries.

Tyler held the berry beside the screen to better compare it to the pictures. "Looks the same," he said. He tilted his head backward. The berry dropped into his mouth. He slowly chewed, and of course, had to dramatically wait to tell us what he thought of it. Finally, he held up his finger. "That tastes like a blueberry to me."

"Great, cuz I'm starving," Katie said, sliding the phone into her pocket.

"Yea, me too," Tyler said.

We all looked for more blueberry plants. The cool thing was, now that we knew what to look for, they were easy to spot. They had been around us the whole time; we just hadn't noticed.

At first, we picked the berries gently. After a while, we just grabbed handfuls and pulled them from the branches, which sometimes squished the berries. Their juices stained our skin a purple color, but it was worth being able to fill our mouths faster.

Chapter 9
This Way

We ate blueberries a long time. When we picked them all in one spot, we moved on to another spot. After we were full, we held onto the bottoms of our shirts and filled a little pouch of blueberries to save for later. Tyler even took his socks off, filled them with berries, and tied them to a belt loop. I'll admit, I was tempted to fill my socks too, but couldn't get over the idea of eating food out of something my feet had been touching.

"Next time, we shouldn't leave the backpack in the canoe," Melisa said. A few berries tumbled out the sides of the bulge in her shirt. "Let's go back."

Now that we were finally ready to go, something funny happened. Katie and I started walking one way, and Melisa and Tyler walked a different way.

"Hey, the trail is this way guys," Melisa called.

"No, it's not," Katie said.

They turned around and glared at each other.

Melisa turned and marched away. "Well, I'm going this way."

Katie did the same, except she walked in the other direction.

Splitting up didn't seem like a good idea. I tried to think fast, but the more I thought about it, the more I realized that I had no clue where we were. I had been concentrating too much on picking berries to pay any attention to where we left the trail.

"Hey, just wait a minute. We need to stick together," I finally said.

Katie turned around and held out one of her arms. "Well, I don't want to get lost just because she doesn't know where she's going."

That comment only made Melisa walk faster. Soon, both girls were out of sight.

"You guys, stop it! Come back," Tyler called to them.

"Fine then, we're staying here until you're ready to work together," I yelled.

Me and Tyler stood there waiting for them to come back. Pretty soon, we stopped waiting for them to come back and started hoping for them to come back. Then we hoped one of them would come back so that we could go look for the other. We even made a bet on who would cave in and come back first. I'm not going to tell you who I bet on. If she found out, I'd have a whole new survival story to write about. That's, *if* I'd survive.

Eventually, we realized neither would come back, so we decided to find the lake ourselves.

"I'm pretty sure we're lost." Tyler said. "And if either of the girls found the trail again, they would've probably told us, so they're probably lost too."

"Probably," I agreed.

I remembered seeing on TV once that woodsmen, back in the old days, could tell what direction they needed to go based on the position of the sun. I looked at the sun, but it didn't help. Well, at least it didn't help until I noticed the tree branches swaying in front of the sun.

"I know. I'll climb a tree," I told Tyler. "If I'm a little higher, I might be able to see the lake. Then we won't need the moose trail."

We found a tree that looked good for climbing, except its lowest branch was too high off the ground for either of us to reach. After a quick brainstorming session, we decided that if Tyler knelt next to the tree, I could stand on his shoulders.

Tyler opened his shirt so that I could dump my berries in with his. Then I climbed onto his shoulders and into the tree. After pulling myself a few branches higher, I could finally see sunlight reflecting off the lake's surface.

Chapter 10
No Bull

It took us a long time to get there, even after we knew which direction to walk. The bushes were thick and scratched at our arms. Finally, we stumbled out of the forest and onto the lake's shoreline.

"Look," Tyler said. He crouched low to the ground.

I glanced in the direction he was pointing. Not too far down the shore was a moose. It was standing in the lake with its head under the water. A moment later, the head lifted revealing a huge set of antlers. Its mouth was moving, chewing something.

We stayed perfectly still until its head went back underwater.

"It's eating seaweed," Tyler whispered.

"Yuck," I said.

"Maybe it's better than you think."

I shook my head. "Not if it tastes anything like it smells."

"What should we do?" Tyler asked.

I looked around for ideas. The best weapon I could find was a rock, so I picked up a few.

"You remember how the App called a moose the 'Giant of the Forest'?"

"Yea," Tyler said.

I handed him a rock. "And you've heard the story of David and Goliath?"

The moose lifted its head out of the water. Some of the weeds were dangling from its antlers.

"But didn't he have a slingshot?" Tyler asked.

"Do you have a better idea?" I asked. "If you want to get close enough to use the pocket knife, be my guest."

"Not really," Tyler admitted.

"Alright, as soon as he puts his head under again, we'll run up to him," I said. "He won't be able to see us that way."

"He's done chewing," Tyler said.

"Wait for it... Wait for it," I whispered. "Go!"

We ran the best we could, while still holding the blueberries in our shirts. Tyler wasn't as fast, and the socks dangling from his pants bounced with each stride he took. Soon, we were right in front of the moose. It just stood there with its head in the water, so we waited for it to surface again.

I actually felt bad for organizing the surprise attack. It just looked like a clueless, helpless animal, but boy was I wrong.

Suddenly, up pops the moose head and after that our memories get a little fuzzy. You see, I swear that the rock I threw hit the moose's antler and bounced into the water, and Tyler's rock simply landed in the water. Tyler says it was the other way around. Either way, we were both unimpressed with how we implemented the attack. And you probably guessed it; the moose was unimpressed too.

Chapter 11
Counter Attack

The moose charged. Lake water sprayed in all directions. For being such a big animal, it sure could move. By the time we realized what was happening, it was halfway to us. It lowered its head and tilted its antlers forward.

"AAAAHHHHHHHHHHHHHHHH!"

I was the first to run back down the shoreline. I glanced over my shoulder in time to see that Tyler was in too much shock to do anything more than stumble backward a few steps. He tripped over the incline of the lake's embankment and landed on his butt in a sitting position. A moment later, the moose trampled over the top of Tyler and that was the end of him. Not a pretty picture with the blood and guts being squished everywhere.

Okay, that didn't really happen. That's just what I thought the moose would do when I looked over my shoulder and saw Tyler fall onto his butt. Instead, the moose bellowed a deep roar, and chased after me.

The moose didn't splash as much in the shallow water. It picked up speed when it reached dry land and gained on me fast. I swerved into the forest and jumped behind a tree. The moose bulldozed past me. It stopped nearby and thrashed its antlers at some bushes. Leaves and twigs literally flung to the ground, and the moose stomped its feet on them.

I scrambled to the other side of a tree, but wished the trunk was wider. The moose stopped thrashing. It looked at me, lowered its head, and let out a deep growl. It was a terrible sound that made the hairs on the back of my neck stand.

Trust me, I didn't know moose could growl either, but this one did.

Still don't believe me? Well, there's a YouTube video you can watch of a mama moose growling at a dog. Scary, I know. You'd expect a sound like that from a bear, not a moose.

While the moose was growling, I was trying to figure out a plan. What I wanted to do was climb the tree, but the moose was too close for that. The beast was probably ten feet tall when you included its antlers. After struggling to climb a tree to find our way back to the lake, I knew there was no way I could climb higher than ten feet in a matter of seconds, and seconds is all I would have.

I stood perfectly still, but was ready to sprint around the tree trunk if it charged again. Not the most comforting plan after seeing how fast the moose could run.

Finally, the moose stopped growling. He held his head high, turned, and lumbered into the forest, as if he thought we were even. I ambushed him with a rock, and he scared the living daylights out of me.

PS: I wonder if moose can feel pain in their antlers. If not, I think it overreacted.

Chapter 12
Not Again

The sound of snapping twigs grew faint. Eventually, I couldn't hear the moose at all.

Tyler was still by the lake, but walking closer to me. One hand held the pocket knife. "Josh, are you O.K.?"

"Yea." I stepped away from the tree. "Don't worry. It's gone," I added, after noticing he was hunching over to look in the forest.

Tyler straightened himself. "That was crazy. It could've killed us." He folded the blade and put the knife back in his pocket.

I didn't want to think about what could've happened. "Let's get back to the canoe," I said.

We walked along the shoreline and passed the place where the moose had first started chasing us. The blueberries that had been in our shirts were scattered across the sand. I hadn't even noticed that I had dropped mine.

We were getting close to the canoe when I thought I heard something. We both stopped.

"You heard it too." I asked.

Tyler nodded.

It was the sound of more twigs breaking and leaves rustling. It was coming from the forest, somewhere in front of us. I sprinted for the canoe, hoping to make it there before the moose stepped out of the woods and found us again.

I grabbed the canoe, pushed it in the lake, and hopped in. Last time we pushed off from shore, Tyler's end of the canoe got stuck in the shallow water. So, I started paddling without him.

"Wait for me," he cried.

Chapter 13
The Sound

I can't say I'm proud of leaving Tyler on shore. That's just how it happened. It was only the second time I had ever truly feared for my life, and the first time had just been a few minutes ago.

You might think that you'd never do something like that. I never thought I would either. Maybe you would've waited for Tyler; maybe you wouldn't have. Nobody really knows what they'd do until they're in a situation like that. All I want to say is, don't judge me. I'm just trying to be honest with you when telling this story.

I only made it a few yards away from shore when Tyler plunged into the water. He grabbed the canoe and tried to climb in. The whole canoe leaned to the side and tipped over instead.

We surfaced and turned to the sound of cracking branches. The lake was only waist deep where we stood. I wiped water from my eyes and waited for the moose to appear. Tyler took a deep breath and vanished under the surface.

"What are you doing?" Katie asked. She stepped out of the forest, right where the noise had been coming from, still holding blueberries in the front of her shirt.

I wasn't sure how to answer. Now that I knew it was only Katie in the woods, I felt relieved, drenched, and silly. Thankfully, I didn't need to.

Tyler popped out of the water about ten yards away. He swam away from shore, arms smacking the lake with each stroke. Every now and then his head turned toward the sky for a gasp of air.

Did he look even more pathetic that I did? Yes, but I was impressed. If it really had been the moose again, he would have been safe, and I would've been trampled into the seaweed.

Chapter 14
The Idea

"Melisaaaaa!" We shouted. Finally, we heard a faint reply.

"Over here. I'm over here."

Tyler pointed to the far side of the lake. "There she is."

Melisa was standing on shore, where we had first appeared, waving one arm above her head to get our attention.

"Let's go," Katie said. She climbed into the canoe but had to wipe water off the back seat before sitting down. "Why do you guys have to be so stupid?" she asked. "Now my jeans are going to be wet."

I didn't feel sorry about her jeans. I did feel sorry about leaving Tyler on shore, so I insisted that he sit on the front seat. I sat in the middle, right where a puddle was forming from all the water drops that were trickling to the center of the canoe.

Melisa laid in the grass while waiting for us. "Told you I knew which way the trail was," she said.

"O.K., I was lost," Katie admitted, as the canoe came ashore.

"So how'd you find your way back then?" Tyler asked.

"You guys were screaming like a bunch of girls," Katie said. "I just followed your voices back to the lake."

"Yea, what was that all about?" Melisa asked.

"We almost got beat-up by a moose," I answered.

"I should have taken a picture of them," Katie said. "The look on Josh's face was priceless."

Melisa sat up straighter. "Wait a minute, your phone has a camera."

Katie rolled her eyes. "Do you think I bought it from a caveman?"

"Maybe that's what the App means when it says that we need to 'shoot' a moose," Melisa said. "You know, like shoot a photo."

Tyler and I looked at each other. That would have been nice to know a half hour ago.

Katie held out a leaf and took a picture of it. There was an electronic click sound. Then a voice came on the phone. It spoke without emotion, like a robot. "Analyzing image," the voice said... "Red Oak," it concluded, a moment later.

Katie smiled. "You really are a wildlife identification app."

Chapter 15
Making Camp

We agreed that tracking an upset moose is a bad idea. Instead, we decided to wait for it to come back to the lake. Then, we would get in the canoe and paddle close enough to take a picture, but stay far enough away to be safe.

While we waited, Katie became obsessed with taking pictures. She took pictures of bushes, and pinecones, and a snail she found by the lake. When a couple birds began chirping in the treetops, she took a picture of them too. The App identified them as a Black-Capped Chickadee and an Ovenbird. They were both birds I've probably seen hundreds of times before, but I'll admit, it was neat to finally know what they're called.

"I wonder how it identifies them," I said.

Melisa shrugged. "Face recognition software is really good these days. It's probably like that, except for plants and animals."

Tyler sat on a log. He untied a sock from his belt loop. The way it drooped made it clear that it was still damp from our little swim. He poured a pile of blueberries into his hand and ate them. "What if it doesn't come back?" he asked.

"It'll come back, but it might take a while," Melisa said, "especially since you guys scared it."

"It didn't look scared to me, just angry," I said.

"Either way it might take a while to get a moose picture," Melisa said. "We should probably prepare to stay here."

"You mean spend the night?" Katie asked.

Melisa held her arms out. "Unless it comes back this evening, I don't think we have a choice."

Tyler put the blueberries back in his sock and leaned it against the log. He started gathering sticks and pine needles. "We'll need a fire," he said.

"And how do you plan to start one?" Katie asked. "You guys drenched our matches. Remember?"

I went to the canoe and grabbed the backpack. The matches felt soggy. I tried to light one, but the head just smeared off.

Tyler picked up a couple rocks and hit them together.

"Only certain rocks make sparks," Melisa told him.

Tyler dropped the rocks and picked up two new ones. "If only we had a magnifying glass."

"If only we had some dry matches and a lighter," Melisa said.

"Maybe you should try rubbing some sticks together." Katie teased.

"Give him a break," I said. "At least he's trying."

"Can I see your glasses?" Tyler asked.

"No way," Melisa said.

Tyler stepped closer to her. "But maybe we could use them like a magnifying glass."

Melisa hesitated. She took her glasses off, but instead of giving them to Tyler, she handed them to me. "Just be careful. OK?"

Without glasses, Melisa looked like a totally different person. She could have even passed as cute. "I will," I promised, and gently took the glasses from her.

I sat next to Tyler's pile of sticks and pine needles. I angled the glasses so the sun passed through them and hit the pile. I tried to center the sunlight by tilting the glasses ever so slightly and moving them closer to the ground. Finally, most of the light began to focus on an area that was smaller than the size of a sesame seed. You know, the kind you find on top of a hamburger bun.

The pine needle underneath the beam of light began to curl and smoke, but the smoke disappeared after a couple seconds. I moved the light to a different pine needle. It did the same thing.

"I'll get some grass," Tyler said.

He set a handful of dead grass under the beam of light. The heat also made them curl and smolder, but the grass kept smoking. Eventually, they burst into flames. The fire grew, burning the grass and some pine needles too. Tyler set a few sticks on top, and I handed the glasses back to Melisa.

Chapter 16
Fire

The sun set beyond the lake. The sky turned from orange to red. Then even the red dimmed away.

Darkness filled the forest. Firelight flickered across Tyler's face. He used the pocket knife to sharpen the end of a stick. He was making spears. I was a little disappointed that we hadn't thought of making spears earlier. It'd be nice to finally have something to protect ourselves with.

A log fell over, causing sparks to swirl above the flames.

"What do you think our parents are thinking?" Tyler asked.

"I bet they're scared," Melisa said. "I wish we could text them. Let them know we're alright."

"My parents probably have a huge search party looking for me," Katie said. "Looking for all of us," she quickly added.

I shook my head. "Like that'll do any good. Nobody's going to be looking for us out here."

The significance of my words stopped our conversation. Nobody had to talk. We were all thinking the same thing. Unless we could find a way home ourselves, nobody would ever find us.

"Come on you guys. We have to stay positive," Melisa finally said. "At least we have a plan now. It's just a matter of time before the moose comes back. We'll take its picture and be home again."

"Starlight, star bright, the first star I see tonight," Katie began. She was staring at the sky. "I wish I may, I wish I might, get the wish I wish tonight."

I looked up. Only sections of the sky could be seen because dark branches hung in the way.

"Can you guys see it," Katie asked. She pointed upward.

"I see it," Tyler said.

"There's two of them," I added.

Can you believe that? We could actually see the stars appearing. For the next few minutes, we each made wishes and pointed out more stars. We stopped when we got to eleven. After that, so many appeared we didn't bother to count anymore.

I don't know where you grew up, but in Columbus, all the lights make it hard to see the stars at night. Sure, you can see plenty of them, but they're never as bright as they looked in the forest, and I had never seen so many in my life.

It had been a long time since I had wished on a star, which is sad when you think about it. That's 365 free wishes a year that I'd been missing. Well, except for cloudy nights. Of course, people can't see stars if clouds are blocking them. Either way, I've probably been wasting hundreds of wishes every year by not taking time to look at the stars.

"Do you know what I've always wanted to do?" Tyler asked.

"No, but I have a feeling you're going to tell us," Katie said.

"Howl at the moon."

"Well thank goodness there's no moon out tonight," Melisa said.

"Well you know what I mean," Tyler said. "Just howl at the sky."

Melisa covered her ears. Tyler tilted his head back. "AWHOOOOOOOOOOoooooooo," he called out. "Come on you guys. Try it," he said. "It makes you feel completely free."

I have to admit, it did sound fun. I tilted my head back and howled too. Tyler howled with me. Even Katie joined in. I don't think Katie really had the urge to howl. She just did it because she knew it would annoy Melisa.

"Join the pack Melisa," I said.

She rolled her eyes and straightened her back. "awhooo."

"Come on," Tyler said.

"It's not like anyone's going to hear us out here," Katie added.

Melisa threw her head back and let out a real howl. "Oww Oww AWWHOOOOOOOO."

We all joined in with her and continued our howls until all the air had been forced from our lungs. Melisa grinned, and we couldn't keep from laughing. Until we heard a different howl. It was soft, eerie, and sent a shiver down my spine. It wasn't super close, probably from the other side of the lake. Even still, it felt like we were being watched. I glanced over my shoulder and tried to peer into the forest, but all I saw was darkness.

Chapter 17
Visitors in the Night

I'll admit that hearing the wolf howl kind of freaked me out. I kept thinking that I could hear something walking in the forest. Sometimes, it sounded like a branch moving and other times it sounded like gravel crunching as something took a step. At first, I was afraid it was a wolf or a bear. Later I imagined that giant moose creeping up on us. I was afraid it might come charging out of the darkness and stomp on us with its huge feet.

As you can probably imagine, all these thoughts made it hard to fall asleep. Eventually, I did go to sleep though. After a while, a person gets so darn tired that it's impossible to stay awake, even if they want to.

The air grew cool during the night. We slept close to the fire to keep warm. When the fire died down to a pile of glowing embers, someone would wake up and add a few more pieces of wood.

When I say someone would wake up, I mean someone besides me. I'm the kind of person that hits the snooze button on their alarm clock a bunch of times before getting up. It was actually just Tyler and sometimes Melisa that put more wood on the fire. I think Katie is a 'hit your alarm clock' kind of person too.

I only got up once during the night. I heard something snarling. Katie let out a loud shriek, and I grabbed the spear Tyler made for me.

"Hey. Hey! That's mine," Tyler yelled.

My eyes focused just in time to see Tyler chasing two raccoons away. The bigger raccoon had one of his blueberry socks in its mouth.

Katie was standing on top of a log, just the way someone would stand on a chair if they saw a mouse on their kitchen floor.

"Well there goes my breakfast," Tyler said, as the thieves ran into the darkness.

Chapter 18
Morning

It was easy to find Tyler's sock in the morning. The dim light on the horizon was all we needed to see it lying on the ground. A hole was torn where the big toe was supposed to go. Threads dangled around the edges of the hole and all of the blueberries were gone. Monkey tracks surrounded the sock.

"Wait a minute," I said. "These have to be raccoon tracks."

"I knew there weren't any monkeys around here," Melisa said.

Katie searched for information in the App, just to double check that they were raccoon tracks. The tracks were a perfect match.

Tyler sat on a log by the fire and put his sock back on. He frowned at the toe sticking out of the hole.

Melisa ran to the lake. "You guys hurry," she said.

The moose was back. It was at the far end of the lake and sticking its head under the water again.

We followed Melisa to the canoe, pushed it in the water, and quietly climbed in. We let Katie sit in the back since she knew how to steer. I sat in front again. I paddled hard but had to slow down, because the paddle made a loud rushing noise through the water. I'd have to be quieter than that if we were going to get close enough for a picture.

We took long slow strokes. The canoe gradually picked up speed. We didn't make a sound as we cruised closer to the moose, except for a gentle "swoosh" each time we dipped a paddle back into the water. This time, the moose saw us coming ahead of time. It stopped eating and watched us glide across the lake.

I could tell by the way the canoe turned in the wrong direction that Katie had stopped steering. I looked back in time to see her pull the phone out of her pocket. She held it up and aimed it at the moose.

The electronic click went off.

"Analyzing image," the robotic voice said.

Chapter 19
Come on Already

Have you ever tripped over something and you knew you were going to fall, but it felt like it took forever for you to actually hit the ground, and the whole time you were wondering how much it's going to hurt when you land? Well, waiting for the image to analyze was sort of like that. It only took a few moments for it to finish, it seemed to take forever, and the whole time I was wondering if it was even going to work.

"Moose... Mission complete," the voice said. "Returning home in one minute..."

I lifted the paddle above my head, "Yea!"

Katie screamed, and Melisa yelled, "WWhhooooHHHooooo."

Tyler for once didn't make noise. He just made a fist and shook it in the air like a boxing champion.

"Returning in 45 seconds..."

The moose looked at us like we were nuts, but it didn't seem to mind us being there. It put its head back in the water to eat. It probably knew that after yesterday, I wouldn't try throwing any more rocks at it.

"High five, high five," Tyler said.

He gave a five to Melisa, who was sitting in the middle of the canoe with him, then gave one to me. Since me and Katie were at the opposite ends of the canoe, we hit our paddles together instead.

"Returning in 30 seconds..."

The moose lifted its head again to chew. Water dripped off of the antlers and made ripples form on the lake's surface.

"Look-it. He's so cute," Melisa said. "I can't believe you guys threw rocks at him."

Yea, she really called it "cute," but I think a better description would be "giant spaz."

"Returning in 15 seconds..."

"Hey, look," Katie said.

She turned the phone around so we could see that the screen was dark again, except for a firefly in the center. Its tail was blinking too.

I wondered if I held onto the paddle hard if it would come home with me. I tightened my grip as the blinking grew brighter.

"Returning in 5... 4... 3... 2... 1..."

The blinking became so bright that the screen began to glow. A pulse of light sprang from the phone, and I had to close my eyes.

Chapter 20
My Eyes Opened

The next moment my eyes opened. I saw that glowing smoke quickly fade away. We were back in Mrs. Emmons' room. The strange thing was, it was like nothing had ever happened, like we had never left. All the other kids were still working at their stations, and Mrs. Emmons was still helping Mark's group unfold hides at the far end of the classroom.

"This is getting weird," I said.

Katie rolled her eyes. "Like it wasn't weird to begin with?"

Melisa raised her hand.

Katie hid the phone in her pocket. "What are you doing?" she asked.

"Mrs. Emmons," Melisa called.

Katie lunged forward and pulled Melisa's arm down. It was too late though. Mrs. Emmons was already on her way over.

Melisa glared at Katie. "What's your problem?" she whispered.

"People will think you're crazy if you tell them."

"You mean they'll think we're crazy," Melisa said.

"No, they'll think **you're** crazy," Katie emphasized. "I'm not going to tell anyone, and I'll say you're nuts when they don't believe you."

"Yes, Melisa?" Mrs. Emmons asked.

Melisa glanced at me. I shook my head, but not enough for others to notice. "Nothing, I... umm... forgot," she said.

"Alright dear, let me know if you remember." Mrs. Emmons walked to a different group that had their hands raised.

Katie took her phone back out. "Help me delete this thing," she said and handed it to Tyler.

"Just show people the pictures you took," Melisa said. "That'll prove to everyone that we're not crazy."

Tyler fiddled with the phone for a while and then shook his head. "There are no pictures," he said. "It must only take pictures so that they can be identified. It doesn't save them."

"The app won't erase either," Tyler added and handed the phone back to Katie. "It's stuck in there."

"O.K., whatever," Katie said. "I just won't click on it again. But you guys need to pretend this whole thing never happened. Deal?"

I nodded.

Tyler looked around the room as if he was checking to see if anyone was listening. "Deal."

We turned to Melisa.

"Alright. Fine," she said, then crossed her arms.

Chapter 21
The End

The end? Ha. Very funny.

I held up my end of the bargain and didn't tell anyone about our little experience. None of the others told either. We acted as if nothing ever happened. Katie hung out with her cool friends, I hung out with Mark, Melisa tried to be a know-it-all for Mrs. Emmons, and Tyler was just Tyler. Then the next day, when everything felt back-to-normal, it happened again.

👍 Next in the Series

Scenes from Book 2

About Moose

Quick Facts

Moose are the largest species of deer.
Height: 5 – 6.5 ft. at the shoulders.
Weight: Often over 1000 pounds.
Antler size: Can be 6 ft. wide and 70 pounds.
Running Speed: Up to 35 mph.

Are Moose Dangerous?

Moose are timid animals that usually hide when they see a human, but they are still very dangerous. According to the U.S. National Park Service, moose injure more people in Alaska than grizzly bears, black bears, and polar bears combined. Bulls are more aggressive during the rutting season and females are very protective of their calves.

Surviving a Moose Encounter

Most attacks occur when moose feel threatened. Keeping your distance and preventing an attack is the best way to survive a moose encounter.

If an attack does occur, run away. Moose are not predators like bears. If you run, chances are they won't chase you very far. Hiding behind something solid like a large rock or tree is another option. Once you no longer appear to be a threat, a moose will usually leave you alone.

Do Moose Really Growl?

Moose are typically quiet. Despite their large size, they can slip through a forest with hardly a sound. Moose can make lots of different noises when they want to. They can grunt, bleat, moan, growl, and roar.

Yes, there really is a YouTube video of a mother moose growling at a dog. I currently have links to this video and other moose sounds on my website.

I've personally heard a moose growl while camping in Minnesota's Boundary Waters Canoe Area. It was extremely loud. I thought a bear was near the campsite until I saw a mother moose and calf nearby and realized it was not a bear after all.

Follow this link to hear a mama moose growl at a dog.

 www.karlsteam.com/books/surviving-moose-lake
(Skip 1 minute 10 seconds into the video.)

Would You Survive the Wild?

Starting a Fire

You can start fires with a pair of glasses, but don't rely on them. If it's cloudy or dark outside, you'll be in trouble. Matches, lighters, and flint stones are better options.

Practice building fires before going into the wilderness because this skill could save your life.

Please don't start a fire without the supervision of a responsible adult, and even then, be very careful.

Don't Get Lost

Getting lost in the wild is easier than you may think, and it's a mistake that has cost many their lives. Staying on designated hiking trails and having a good map are the best ways to make sure this doesn't happen to you.

Make sure to bring that map even if you plan on using the GPS on your cell phone. Phones can lose reception, run out of batteries, get lost, broken, whatever.

If You Do Get Lost

Unfortunately, every situation is different. Sometimes, it's best to stay where you are and wait for help. Other times, you may be able to figure out where you are. For instance, if you remember that there was a highway to the east, it may be better to walk in that direction until you find the road.

The main thing is to stay calm. Panicking often leads to poor decisions. Depending on your circumstances, you may want to create a help signal, build a fire, find water, or seek shelter.

Edible Plants

Be very careful about eating wild plants. Unless you know what you're doing, you might accidentally eat something poisonous. Take the time to learn what can and cannot be eaten before you ever find yourself in an emergency.

Food and Water

Believe it or not, you can live a few weeks without eating, but only a few days without water. That's why water should be your priority.

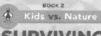

Kids vs. Nature

SURVIVING
DESERT VIEW

Written by
KARL STEAM

Kids vs. Nature

SURVIVING
HORSE ISLAND

Written by
KARL STEAM

Kids vs. Nature

SURVIVING
COUGAR MOUNTAIN

Written by
KARL STEAM

Kids vs. Nature

SURVIVING
CRYSTAL CAVERN

Written by
KARL STEAM

Kids vs. Nature

SURVIVING
CROCODILE SWAMP

Written by
KARL STEAM

Kids vs. Nature

RAPIDS
CANYON

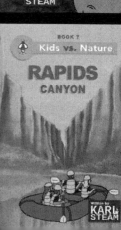

Written by
KARL STEAM

For those who love the outdoors.

ISBN: 978-1-63578-006-2

Current contact information for Libro Studio LLC can be found at www.LibroStudioLLC.com

Image Credits:
hxdbzxy/Shutterstock.com (pages 4, 9, 68, 69)
Jeff Holcombe/Shutterstock.com (pages 11, 12, 15)
Emily P-K/Shutterstock.com (page 20)
Andrzej Puchta/Shutterstock.com (page 22)
Elena Elisseeva/Shutterstock.com (page 24, 45)
Grisha Bruev/Shutterstock.com (page 26)
Fineart1/Shutterstock.com (page 28)
basel101658/Shutterstock.com (page 31)
www.sandatlas.org/Shutterstock.com (pages 33, 34)
Voronin76/Shutterstock.com (page 36)
Brian Lasenby/Shutterstock.com (pages 38, 40)
Tom Tietz/Shutterstock.com (page 42)
Bildagentur Zoonar GmbH/Shutterstock.com (page 47)
Maksym Holovinov/Shutterstock.com (page 50)
NataliaL/Shutterstock.com (page 54)
Cara A. Davis/Shutterstock.com (page 57, 75)
eddtoro/Shutterstock.com (page 61)
Sebastien Burel/Shutterstock.com (page 66)
Vlad Ageshin/Shutterstock.com (page 72)
WorldWide/Shutterstock.com (page 72)

Made in the USA
Middletown, DE
19 June 2021